The
First
Betrayal

A Prequel Novelette to
The Hand of Maud

Patti A. Pierucci

INKSPIRE
PRESS

The First Betrayal
A Prequel Novelette to The Hand of Maud

By Patti A. Pierucci

ISBN #: 979-8-9994463-8-1

Book cover design: InkSpire Press

Author's Note: This is a work of fiction. Names, events, and characters (including real-life historical figures and events) are either entirely imaginary or are used fictitiously.

For my Son, Patrick Aaron Russell

PROLOGUE

Normandy, 1139

The wind clawed at the shutters of the fortress, rattling them like dry bones. Inside, the air was damp and cold, the chamber lit by no more than two torches. Their flames bent sideways with each draft that snaked through the stone, sending shadows leaping across the walls.

At the table sat Empress Matilda—widow of the Holy Roman Emperor, daughter of England's late King Henry I, and by right his chosen heir. Yet the crown that should have rested on her head now rested on the head of her cousin, Stephen of Blois. When Henry had died, the very barons who once swore their fealty to her had thrown their support to Stephen instead. England, her inheritance, had been stolen.

Matilda, though, was not a woman to bow. She was steely beneath her rich velvet gown, with a will sharpened in the courts of emperors, tempered by exile and loss. Though she commanded only a few loyal men, though her fortune was meager, she carried with her something stronger than parchment claims and oaths easily broken.

She had a relic.

On the table between her and her half-brother, Robert of Gloucester, lay a golden hand, palm upraised as if in benediction, its surface sparkling with jewels. Diamonds, rubies, sapphires, and emeralds sparkled in the firelight. Even in the dimness, the hand glowed as though it held its own flame.

Robert folded his arms, his face etched with worry. "When you cross into England, men will call you a pretender. They will call you foreign." His voice hardened. "They will call you a woman. But with this relic, they will call you the chosen heir to the throne."

In the corner, the goldsmith shifted uneasily. His stained hands clutched a rag, his shoulders stooped, seemingly beneath the weight of secrets being discussed before him. For weeks he had labored at Matilda's command, crafting a second hand, a perfect twin. His voice trembled as he spoke.

"My lady, forgive me, but the copy is not what the true one is. The metal is but a copper alloy, gilded with leaf. The stones are glass and enamel. To most eyes it will glitter, but at a closer gaze—"

Matilda cut him off with a sharp look. "It need not endure forever. It need only buy us time, should the true relic fall into unworthy hands."

Robert leaned forward, his tone low and grim. "And it will fall, Maud. All relics do. Men covet them and kill for them. If thieves seize one, let them boast of the false hand while the true remains hidden."

The goldsmith swallowed hard and bowed. "Then may God grant you favor, for this task is perilous. Should word spread that I—"

"You will speak of this to no one," Robert snapped. "If your tongue betrays you, this will be the last service you perform."

The goldsmith's courage wavered, but his hands remembered what to do. He drew a deep breath, then stepped to the bench, tapping a bundle no bigger than a prayer book. "This is how I did it," he said, his voice low. "Brass and copper, hammered thin and shocked in vinegar. Leafed in gold, burnished with a dog's tooth till it lied like sunlight. The stones? Paste—fire-colored, wheel-cut, dressed to pass for truth under a torch."

He lifted a narrow tool, its point no thicker than a thorn. "For the true one, as you commanded, my lady—here is the mark no man would know to seek." He traced the underside of the true Hand's wrist, where the gold was smooth. "A craftsman's cross, no bigger than a flea."

Robert's mouth tightened. "And if a thief looks?"

"Then God grant him poor candlelight," the goldsmith said, with a flicker of humor. "A man sees what he wants to see. The jewels will attract all eyes first, not the craftsman's cross—or lack of it."

Matilda's bright gaze never left the counterfeit relic. "Then let all of England see," she said. "And let those who would steal learn that even the brightest gold can deceive."

Matilda reached for the relic, lifting it in both hands. The torchlight caught the jeweled palm and sent beams of color scattering across the chamber like a rainbow.

"My father named me his heir," she said, her voice steady, each word the weight of her determination. "Stephen stole what was mine. But England will see, with this true Hand, that heaven's blessing is not his but mine. I will not bend, and I will not break. England is mine, and I'm coming to claim it."

She kissed the golden fingers on the Hand as if they belonged to a lover. But in doing so, she was sealing her oath.

Outside, the storm broke fully, lashing the walls with rain. At dawn she would sail, carrying both relics—the true and the false—hidden in her baggage. And with them, the seed of the legend of the Hand of Maud.

CHAPTER ONE

The Empire's Bride

They were wed in Mainz, Germany, beneath soaring church vaults, a girl with a queen's name bound to a man who wore an empire like his armor. Matilda stood very straight, as she had been taught, while Henry, Emperor of the Romans, took her hand. He was not unkind; he was simply a mountain—large, cold, immovable.

The court called her Königin, the German word for empress. Wealthy women in fur-trimmed sleeves taught her which finger to lift at which benediction, which step to take at which hymn. She learned the ceremony so thoroughly that it ran through her like it was in her life's blood: where to stand, when to bow, how to command with silence and a stare.

At night there was the other lesson, the one feared by young brides. Henry was dutiful there as well—no more, no less. He gave her the kind of gifts that kings gave their queens: a jeweled cross, a delicate crown of silver and pearls, an illuminated book in German which she couldn't read. He gave her, too, the gift of asking nothing of her mind or her heart. It left her free to be molded into what it would one day become: a furnace of duty and resolve.

Years passed in processions and councils. She knelt by altars wherever she traveled, rode at a measured pace through towns where the bells rang and the faces were wary of the foreign girl. She listened while men disputed law with more heat than they ever spent on their women. She held Henry's seal when he needed a steady hand, received petitions from the poor.

On certain days, Henry would set a golden hand-shaped relic near the royal regalia—an old gift from an ancient ruler—and told her, almost smiling, "A ruler's blessing is given with the hand, but it is the wrist that bears the weight of the hand." She remembered. The hand blesses; the wrist aches.

As a young bride crowned Queen of the Romans, Matilda learned power by using it. When her husband, the Holy Roman Emperor, rode to battle or to negotiate with foreign princes, he left her to keep order as his regent—sitting on the throne with the imperial seal at her elbow, presiding over councils, hearing petitions from bishops and burghers, issuing rulings on tiresome quarrels that could topple towns if mishandled. She signed charters, counted revenues, and discovered the quiet exhilaration of taking command—how the room stilled when she spoke, and how the law moved simply because she willed it.

In those absences of the Emperor she was more than an ornament to the throne; she was the keeper of the realm. That taste of undisputed authority took root in her like a strong tree. Sometimes she would think, deep in her soul, that she was born to rule.

Then came the year 1120 and a courier from a faraway place. He told the tale in a whisper that grew: a bright ship, a drunken night, a prince laughing at the ship's railing, and then black water swallowing everything. William Adelin, Matilda's brother, her father Henry I's only legitimate son, was gone with the crew and half of the Norman baronage.

Matilda shut her chamber door and pressed her forehead to the cool stone. Grief came first, hard and clean. He had been proud and foolish and young, and now he was none of those things because he was dead. But she had loved him. When she had exhausted her tears, another feeling rose up from a darker place—a flicker that she crushed with both hands but could not quite kill. *If not he ... then perhaps I.*

Her husband found her there and stood for a time without speaking. "Your father will name an heir," he said at last. "Kings do not like chance or angry barons to choose their successors."

"He will name me," she answered defiantly, like a challenge.

Henry studied her with that mountain look. "Then learn from me how to be a ruler. Learn it until it consumes all of you, body and soul."

In the years that followed, she did exactly that. When her husband rode to subdue a city, she kept order behind him. When he bargained with bishops, she watched which concessions cost him and which he gave gladly. She learned what mercy could buy and what only a sword could hold. And when at last the Emperor died and the imperial court recited prayers over his body, she did not weep in public. She had her learning and her pride. And with the dignity of one who has shouldered heavy responsibilities, she went home.

Her father met her and swore to name her his heir. He staged the swearings of the barons, who knelt and said *fiat*—"let it be done"—but the words rang hollow, like coins clattering to the floor. They all swore their fealty in 1127 and again in 1131, and both times she read the calculation in their eyes. Oaths, she had learned, are not gifts. They are bills that always come due.

When she crossed at last to England in rain that seemed bent on driving her back into the sea, she brought with her all that the Empire had taught: how to command a hall filled with people with stillness, how to turn an insult with a glance, how to endure a loveless marriage without becoming a woman who could not love. And in her baggage, wrapped in wool beneath her other things, she carried a golden hand that had once served as imperial regalia and now would serve another higher purpose.

Beside it, the impostor hand.

She was done being promised what was her rightful place in England. She had come to collect.

CHAPTER TWO

Arrival in a Broken Realm

The coast of England was gray and drenched with rain when the Empress landed. The sea tossed her forth with little grace, and the rain that greeted her seemed determined to send her back into the waves. But Matilda—Maud, as she was called by the French—did not flinch. She sat tall in her saddle, her cloak soaked through, her eyes fixed on the coast, toward the crown that had once rested on her father's head.

England itself bore the scars of Stephen's betrayal. Villages along the road stood hollow and blackened, their thatched roofs charred by fire. In the fields, weeds grew thick where wheat should have ripened. Peasants with hollow cheeks crouched in doorways, their eyes wary and lifeless.

Yet Maud had not crossed the Channel to weep for her inheritance. She had come to claim it.

Once landed, they passed a village where the church bell had fallen and lay cracked in the weeds. A woman stood in a ruined doorway with a child on her hip, sunken-eyed, her hair matted. She did not curtsey. She only watched the riders with the vacant look of the starving.

"Do they know me?" Maud asked softly.

"They know war," Robert said. "It devours everything, even their hunger."

Maud's mouth tightened. "Then let them learn my name again."

A mile farther on, a flock of refugees trudged single file—old men bowed like reeds, boys hauling a cart, a girl with raw hands gripping a rope that dragged an ox. Maud reined in long enough to give the girl her waterskin. The girl stared, astonished, then snatched a sip and fled as if kindness were a ghost that could reach out and harm her.

"Matilda," Robert murmured, riding at her side, "they will call you Maud here. The name sits easier in English mouths."

She sighed a breath that sounded like a laugh. "Then Maud I am. Let the crown come by any name."

The party of John Marshal soon joined them. Maud watched him from the corners of her eyes. He bowed deep, spilled sweet words, and smiled with eyes cold and sharp as a knife. She saw the way his men looked to him—hungry men, men who would not step out of line for fear their leader would throw them to the wolves.

"My lady," John said, his voice smooth as cream, "I am yours in all things. My sword, my men, my house—all for your cause."

Beside her, Robert of Gloucester shifted in his saddle. He knew John for the fox he was: a man who bent with the wind, whose loyalty could be bartered like figs in a market. Yet Maud's face betrayed nothing. She inclined her head in cool acknowledgment.

That night, the company found lodging in a half-ruined manor house, its beams blackened by fire, its walls damp with mildew.

Robert drew close. "Stephen will test our walls," he warned Maud.

"He will not get through," Maud said. But she tightened her fingers around the thought of the Hand, and for the first time since crossing the sea she felt the old chill of a court where a smile could be more like a sharp knife than a soft caress.

Smoke curled from torches set into the cracked stone of the manor house as Matilda summoned her most trusted knight, Sir Geoffrey de Morville.

He entered weary, mud clinging to his boots, his broad shoulders sagging, yet his gaze was steady. Upon the table lay the relic, unwrapped at last. The jeweled hand caught the light, scattering sparks of red, green, and blue.

"This is the Hand of the Holy Roman Empire," Matilda declared, her voice filling the hall. "Bequeathed to me by my lord, Emperor Henry, before his death. It is heaven's sign, the seal of my right to rule. With this I shall win the people's hearts and the crown that is mine. England will see that God Himself favors my cause."

She turned to Geoffrey, her expression hardening. "You will guard it with your life. Let no thief, no traitor, ever lay a hand upon it. For if I lose this relic, I lose more than treasure. I lose England."

Geoffrey went down on one knee. "By my sword, by my blood, by my soul, I will not fail you."

The Hand's jeweled palm seemed to gleam brighter at his vow, as though heaven itself bore witness.

Sir Geoffrey felt the weight of the relic before it even passed into his keeping. Not only gold. Not only jewels. It carried the burden of a crown—and the envy of men who would kill for it.

He rose and spoke, his voice resolute. "I will guard this—your Hand of Maud—with my life."

What neither of them knew was that hidden in the shadows lingered John Marshal, his eyes gleaming, his smile widening with every word he overheard.

CHAPTER THREE

The Theft

The rain had not eased since Maud's landing. Day after day it battered the road, turning fields into bogs and filling wagon ruts with puddles. The Empress's small army pressed inland nonetheless, heading toward Oxford where Maud hoped Robert might gather men to her banner.

Sir Geoffrey rode close to the baggage wagons, his cloak soaked. Beneath one tarp lay the burden that pressed harder on him than the steel of his chainmail: the Hand of Maud, wrapped in wool and locked in a chest. Even unseen, he could see its gleaming brilliance in his mind. He had sworn to guard it with his life.

Sleep came fitfully to him these nights. Each gust of wind sent him listening for footsteps. Each crack of a branch or creak of leather made his hand fly to the hilt of his sword. He had fought in wars before yet never carried such a weight upon his soul.

On the third night, another storm came howling.

The gale ripped at the tents, snapping ropes, sending canvas whipping into the black sky. Horses screamed, straining against their tethers as hail pelted their flanks. Men shouted through the downpour, their torches sputtering and dying in the wind. Sir Geoffrey staggered from his pallet, snatched his sword, and sprinted toward the wagons.

Lightning split the night, and for an instant the whole camp was lit as if on fire. Geoffrey saw it clearly: one of the chests yawning open, its iron fittings broken apart. A guard sprawled in the mud, groaning, another stiff and face down on the ground, with rain streaming across his dead body.

The wrappings were gone. The Hand of Maud had vanished. God help the man who took it.

"Alarm!" Geoffrey roared. His voice was barely heard over the storm. "The Hand is gone!"

Chaos soon erupted. Men stumbled half-armed from their shelters, some barefoot, some clutching shields in confusion. Oaths and curses mingled with prayers. Panic spread as quickly as fire in a straw-filled barn.

Robert of Gloucester suddenly appeared, rain streaming from his hood, his face set grim. "What is it? What's been taken?"

Geoffrey forced the words through clenched teeth. "The Hand."

For a heartbeat there was silence, then a dozen men crossed themselves at once. Whispers tore through the ranks: God's judgment. An ill omen. We are undone.

Through the confusion came John Marshal. Unlike the rest, he was mounted, his horse stamping in the mud. His cloak hung suspiciously dry, as though he had been waiting, not struggling in the storm like the other men. His tone was smooth, carrying just enough to be heard by too many ears.

"Bad fortune, Sir Geoffrey. Perhaps heaven has reclaimed what mortal hands should never hold."

Geoffrey spun, fury flashing. "This was no act of heaven. Men did this—men who knew where to strike, who used the storm as their cloak."

John's smile widened, foxlike. "If you suggest treachery, name your traitor. For myself, I never believed such a relic was safe in your keeping."

Robert stepped between them, his voice sharp. "Enough. Sir Geoffrey has never broken an oath. Can all here say the same?" His eyes lingered on John, who only smirked in return.

Geoffrey's heart hammered. "My lord," he said to Robert, his voice steady despite the storm's unrelenting drive, "give me men. I will ride after it and bring it back. If I fail, then let me fall on my sword."

Robert studied him, then nodded. "Take a small company. Too many and you will be seen. Find it, Geoffrey. Without the Hand, my sister's cause may die, and the realm will be in the hands of a usurper."

Geoffrey bowed. "By my life, I will not fail."

As he turned to gather his men, John Marshal leaned down from the saddle, his eyes gleaming like a predator caught in the light. His words were soft but meant for Geoffrey alone.

"Bold vows," he murmured. "But boldness is no shield against the swords of men who lust for gold. Remember that, Sir Geoffrey."

"Men like yourself?" Sir Geoffrey spat. "Perhaps my search should begin with your tent."

"By all means," said John Marshal, waving his arm toward his tent to usher him in. "Don't steal anything yourself while you're in there."

Furious, Geoffrey swung into the saddle, rain lashing his face. The storm swallowed him and his men as they rode into the night. Yet in his heart he knew this theft had been no chance raid. The Hand had been hunted. And the fox who prowled their own camp seemed to be smiling at the thought of it.

CHAPTER FOUR

Between Storm and Steel

The storm blew itself out by morning, but the land it left behind was scarred, wounded. Sir Geoffrey rode with six men, following the thieves' hoofprints where they could—ripped turf at a ford, a snapped tree switch, a smear of blood on a gatepost where some careless rider scraped his knee.

A cottage door stood open to the rain. Inside, a woman fed a fire with damp kindling. Her face was dirty and gaunt.

"Have you seen riders?" Geoffrey asked, pushing back his hood.

She nodded once. "A cart in the night. Wheels wrapped in sacking against the stones. Men riding close about it, keeping their torches low."

Geoffrey's jaw tightened. "How many?"

"Half a dozen at least. The cart came near sunset, quiet as cats. Then another knot of horsemen later, no cart—riding fast, as if they meant to guard the road north."

Outside, Geoffrey studied the churned-up yard. Heavy ruts angled toward the king's highway, with narrow hoofprints weaving close beside them. One company of thieves in two parts:

a cart bearing treasure, and horsemen clearing the path ahead.

"Marshal's men, and others beside him. A conspiracy."

"Sir?" asked young Martin, one of his men.

"Nothing," Geoffrey said. "Mount up."

By noon they found a body lashed upright to a tree. A camp groom—Geoffrey knew the lad's face, had seen him brushing down Maud's palfrey two days before. The blue stitches of her livery still clung to his torn sleeve. A strip of parchment fluttered at his chest, stuck to his tunic by blood.

Geoffrey tugged it free and read: *Some treasures do not wish to be kept.*

He stared at the boy's slack face. Had Marshal's men slain him to mock Maud? Or had other forces silenced him for knowing too much? Worse still—had the boy betrayed them, and his killers left him here as warning? Geoffrey's gut twisted. Either way, Maud's camp was bleeding from within as well as without.

Geoffrey burned the scrap of paper without reading it twice. And he thought of John Marshal's dry cloak in a drowning storm.

CHAPTER FIVE

A Hostage and Honor

The trail of the thieves was plain enough: churned mud where hooves had made their mark, broken branches along the forest edge, the stink of sweat of men left in haste. Sir Geoffrey and his men pressed hard, through villages half-abandoned and fields left to rot.

The land itself told the story of England's ruin. Cottages sagged, their doors hanging loose, their hearths cold. Peasants crouched like ghosts among ruins, their faces hollow, too weak to beg. One old woman raised her hand in blessing as Geoffrey passed, her eyes fixed on the sword at his hip. The relic was gone, yet still the people looked to knights for deliverance.

By dusk on the third day, the tracks drew them toward a broad encampment flying Stephen's banners. Smoke rose from a hundred cookfires, and the air was thick with the stench of horse and man. Geoffrey reined in, his jaw tight. If the relic had found its way here, then recovering it would demand boldness— or negotiation.

He entered under a promise of truce, his sword sheathed, his cloak stiff with dried mud. Guards led him past wagons and stables into the heart of the camp. He had expected grim silence, but instead he heard laughter—high, childish laughter.

In the yard a boy of perhaps five swung a stick like a sword, jabbing at a weary knight's leg. The men around him laughed as he shouted, "I'll be the greatest knight in all England!"

Geoffrey stopped, startled. "Who is he?" he asked the soldier at his side.

The man spat into the mud. "John Marshal's whelp. Young William. A hostage of the Bishop for his father's oath." His sneer was bitter. "Not that John keeps oaths. The King threatened to hang the boy, but the lad's too spirited, too merry. Even Stephen could not stomach it."

Geoffrey's gut twisted. He had seen black treachery before, but few fathers would leave a child as ransom while they schemed elsewhere. That was John Marshal all over—evil-hearted, shameless.

The boy turned, catching Geoffrey's eye. His grin was fearless. He raised his stick in salute as if greeting a fellow knight. For an instant, Geoffrey saw not a child but a spark—something that might blaze into greatness one day.

"God keep you, little one," Geoffrey murmured, scarcely aware he had spoken.

The moment passed. Trumpets blared, and Stephen's captains approached. At their center walked the Bishop of Ely, robes trailing, his face as hard as stone. In his hands he carried a golden hand, palm open, jewels blazing in torchlight.

The camp stirred. Men craned forward. Geoffrey's breath caught. Here was the relic.

"This," the Bishop proclaimed, his voice cutting the night, "is the Hand of Maud, delivered to Stephen, the rightful king. Let heaven argue that with that."

Laughter rippled through the ranks. Some mocked Sir Geoffrey, others crossed themselves in awe. Geoffrey stood frozen, fury swelling in his throat. If he returned to Maud empty-handed, her cause would die and Stephen the usurper would cement his rule.

The boy William continued to grin at the assembly, swinging his stick as if he had won some invisible duel.

Geoffrey straightened, his voice steady. "I will bring back what I was sworn to guard. And God Himself may judge which ruler sits on the throne."

The Bishop's eyes narrowed, sharp as a hawk. Behind him, William laughed aloud, fearless, his stick flashing in the torchlight.

And Geoffrey knew this: whatever the cost, he could not fail.

CHAPTER SIX

The Fox Unmasked

The sight of the Bishop's relic haunted Geoffrey as he rode back to the Empress's camp. His mind replayed the boy William's fearless grin, the Bishop's cold pronouncement, and the glitter of jewels.

But darker still was the memory of John Marshal, mounted and waiting in the storm, his cloak dry while others drowned in rain. Geoffrey knew a fox's track when he saw it.

The rain had eased, leaving the camp sodden and gray. Geoffrey pushed into the circle of men where John Marshal stood, his dark eyes sharp beneath a wet fringe of hair, his cloak, now soaked, held in his arms.

"You rode last night," Geoffrey said flatly.

Marshal's mouth twisted. "I ride every night, de Morville. And most mornings, too, if it suits me."

"You were with the Bishop's cart." Geoffrey stepped closer, voice low so the others would not hear. "You know what it carried."

Marshal studied him for a beat, then gave a short laugh. "Aye, I know. I was there when we took it." His teeth flashed.

"But I don't have it now."

Geoffrey's hand brushed the pommel of his sword. "Then who does?" Geoffrey already knew the answer.

"The Bishop." Marshal's tone was mocking. "Wrapped in his holy silks, clutching it like a dog with a bone. You think I'd trust you with that news? You think Maud will thank you for hearing it?"

"You've betrayed her," Geoffrey said, anger tightening his throat. "You've betrayed your oath."

Marshal's eyes narrowed, and he tilted his head toward the men at his back. "And what will you do with that knowledge, de Morville? Ride crying to the Empress?"

Geoffrey's heart thudded with rage. He had his answer: Marshal had ridden with the Bishop. Together they conspired to steal the Hand. Geoffrey also knew that Marshal meant to silence him. His blade slid free, and he called over his shoulder, "Martin, to me!"

Marshal raised his hand and instantly his henchmen were on top of them. The camp erupted with the clash of iron and the cries of men. Geoffrey fought like a man possessed, cutting through one assailant, then another, blood stinging his eyes where a blade grazed his brow.

Geoffrey's strength did not falter. His arm burned, his grip slipped, but he drove through it anyway—steel bit cloth, then flesh. John's howl split the rain.

John staggered back and cursed, his eyes blazing with hatred. "You will pay for that, de Morville."

But Geoffrey and the Empress's men were already claiming victory. John Marshal, wounded and clutching his arm, ordered his men to lay down their weapons.

"Chain them up!" yelled Geoffrey to the Empress's soldiers as he leapt onto his horse and rode into the night air. The cold wind struck his sweat-soaked face like a blessing. He was wounded, but he was victorious.

The Hand of Maud was still not secure, resting in the clutches of the Bishop. He would find a way to get it back from the idling, fat-bellied prelate. His horse threw large clumps of mud behind him as it galloped.

And he swore into the night: *I will not fail.*

CHAPTER SEVEN

The Bishop's Procession

They chose a market town for the spectacle—a place with a square broad enough to hold a thousand people. Rain had washed the streets clean for once, and the apprentices had been warned to keep their elbows in. Banners went up on door lintels. The air smelled of wet wool and vegetables—and a hope that people could not name.

Sir Geoffrey stood by the sidelines, hidden beneath the eaves of a blacksmith. Today he was not a knight renowned for his courage and fierceness in battle. He was nobody at all. Beside him his young man Martin jostled and gawked.

"Be still," Geoffrey murmured. "Watch the spectacle."

The Bishop of Ely entered with choirboys and a ring of men in chainmail. He moved like a ship at sea—bulky and slow, imposing, impossible to ignore—while two clerks carried a chest between them and a third swung the censer. Ely mounted the church steps as if they belonged to him.

"My children," he cried, "God does not leave the righteous without signs."

The chest opened. A golden hand rose into the light. Jewels

winked. There was a sound from the crowd like a low animal hum—the noise a starving peasant makes when seeing food within reach.

Ely held the relic high, palm turned toward the people. "Behold! The Hand of Maud, now the Hand of Stephen, whom God and Church anoint as England's rightful king. Heaven bears witness!"

A woman cried out near the steps, clutching a boy whose leg dragged. The Bishop's eyes sharpened. He beckoned with the open palm of the Hand as if the relic itself commanded him to. "Bring the child."

It was rehearsed; Geoffrey saw it at once. The people made way and the choir struck a note without waiting to be told. Ely touched the Hand's jeweled fingers to the boy's brow, then to the dragging leg, then traced a cross in air.

"Walk," Ely said, loud enough for the farthest hedge to hear.

The boy walked. Badly, with the exaggerated lilt of a child who wants to please men with threatening swords. His mother sobbed and wailed theatrically. The square erupted into whispers that raced from mouth to mouth like hens clucking in a coop: A sign. A blessing. A proof.

Ely raised the relic again, and now there were shouts for Stephen and shouts for God, and some, whose throats did not know which name to choose, shouted both.

"Best bend the knee," a broad-jawed man muttered. "If God's on his side, we'll feel His boot soon enough."

Geoffrey took it all in. He watched the Bishop's performance instead of listening to his words. His empty hand kept reaching for the sword that wasn't there. *You've taken a lie and tried to make it the truth,* Geoffrey thought, *then you covered it in gold and gems. And now you mean to use Empress Maud's own lords as the gild that makes the lie shine.*

The procession moved on. A few coins were tossed by the Bishop's men to make the poor in the crowd grateful—enough only to buy a few loaves of bread. By the time Ely reached the far end of the square, the town had decided to be persuaded, an easy decision when a priest tells you that heaven prefers it.

"Sir," said Martin, "what shall we do?"

Geoffrey answered, "I have seen a display of lies today that would shame a common thief—all of them coming from a man who claims to speak for God. I'm ready to expose those lies."

They eased themselves out of the crowd while the choirboys' voices rose and the censer smoked and the Bishop smiled piously. Geoffrey kept walking until the square was behind him. He did not look back.

CHAPTER EIGHT

The Bishop's Loss

That night, with the Bishop now detached from Stephen's camp and traveling with his own entourage, Geoffrey paid a visit with Martin at his side.

The Bishop of Ely received him like a spider greets a fly, draped in silks and self-satisfaction. "So, Sir Geoffrey, the Empress grows weary of her toys? You've tired of her cause at last?"

Geoffrey inclined his head, letting his shoulders sag as though burdened with defeat. "My lady has few friends left. The lords' oaths bend like reeds in the wind, and she clings to shadows. I will not sink with her."

The Bishop chuckled, fingers tapping the arm of his chair. "A wise admission. You are not the first to come seeking firmer ground."

"I seek more than ground," Geoffrey said, his voice dropping to a confidential rasp. "I seek a master who rewards loyalty. The Empress—she grants words and promises. You, my lord, you hold a relic that commands men's souls." His eyes flicked, almost carelessly, toward the golden Hand resting on a table between them.

The Bishop's gaze sharpened. "So you covet the holy thing?"

Geoffrey allowed a thin smile, the kind a beaten man wears when admitting his hunger. "I covet a cause that will not end at the gallows. If the relic proves your strength, then I would stand where strength stands."

The Bishop leaned forward, his voice low and testing. "And what would you give, Sir Geoffrey, to stand in such a place?"

"My sword, my counsel, my silence," Geoffrey replied smoothly. "Name your enemies, and I will name their weak points. Bid me ride, and I will ride."

For a long moment the Bishop studied him, searching for cracks. Then he reclined with a satisfied sigh. "Perhaps God Himself has delivered you to my tent. Remain here tonight. Tomorrow, I shall find you a task worthy of your zeal."

Geoffrey bowed deeply, hiding the spark in his eyes. As he rose, he caught Martin's gaze from across the tent. His aide's look said everything: the relic was within reach—and the Bishop, blind with pride, had just invited his own undoing.

Geoffrey bowed low, masking the anger that burned in his chest. "Yes, God did indeed deliver me to your tent," he murmured after leaving the Bishop's tent.

Around a campfire that night, a goblet was pressed into Geoffrey's hand, then another, and another. The King's soldiers laughed as the knight swayed on his stool, his words slurred with feigned drunkenness. He sprawled across the rushes, laughing as though overcome by wine.

But when the camp fell still, when only the watch-fires burned and snoring filled the tents, Geoffrey's eyes snapped open. Martin crouched beside him.

"You've fooled them well, my lord," Martin whispered. "I saw you pouring out your wine on the ground when their eyes were diverted. The Bishop has kept the Hand in his tent—on the table by his bed."

Geoffrey rose, shaking the stench of wine from his tunic. "Then we'll not sleep until it is ours."

They moved like shadows between the tents. A loose horse whinnied at the edge of camp—Martin's doing—drawing the guards away. Geoffrey slipped inside the Bishop's pavilion. The air reeked of incense and stale wine. The plump Bishop lay on his pallet, snoring drunkenly. The golden hand gleamed faintly in the dark as it sat on the table.

The fool, thought Geoffrey, *to leave it unguarded while he passed out from too much wine, food, and greed.*

For a moment Geoffrey just stared at the relic, heart thundering. Then, swift as a thief, he snatched it, wrapped it in a length of cloth, and pressed it into Martin's waiting arms outside.

"Never let it out of your sight," he breathed.

They fled into the night, silent as deer. Twice they reined in, still as the dead, as patrols passed by, the relic well hidden. A shout rose in the distance—someone had found the horse loose. By the time suspicion turned toward the Bishop's tent, Geoffrey and Martin were already beyond their reach, their horses moving quickly through the forest.

Geoffrey, breath ragged, allowed himself a grim smile. "The Bishop will wake to find his prayers for wealth and power unanswered."

Martin, who had secured the bundle beneath his cloak, laughed with him.

The two spurred their horses into the dark, leaving behind the campfires of Stephen's men and carrying with them a relic that could tip the fate of England.

(

CHAPTER NINE

The Trial of the Relic

The Hand of Maud and the Bishop—brought at the point of Geoffrey's sword—now lay upon the table, its jeweled palm raised. Torches sputtered in the hall, their flames reflected in ruby, emerald, sapphire, and gold. Around them gathered the lords of Maud's cause, their voices rising in murmurs and suspicion.

Maud, with Robert of Gloucester behind her, strode into the hall with the majesty of a queen. In her hand was the Hand of Maud ... another Hand!

Sir Geoffrey stood bruised and bloodied, every wound burning. He had fought like a man damned to reclaim the relic, yet here was another—one taken from the hands of the Bishop of Ely, the other in the hands of his Empress.

It made no sense—until the pieces fell together.

The storm. The raided chest at Maud's camp. The guards cut down. The Bishop's henchmen, in conspiracy with John Marshal, must have struck there, seizing a false relic. Or was it?

Two relics. Which was the real one?

Robert's voice cut through the murmurs. "The Bishop's

men boast they seized the relic in the storm. Yet Geoffrey here swore an oath and bled to bring one back." Robert looked at the Bishop, who bore the face of a man defeated. He stood slumped, his head hanging.

Robert continued. "If two relics exist, only one can be true." The Bishop flushed crimson. "Lies! This hand came into King Stephen's camp by divine favor. The other is a forgery!"

John Marshal leaned in, his smirk wolfish. "A forgery, perhaps—but forged by whom? Who but the Empress herself would dare such sacrilege?"

A ripple of shock swept the hall. Men muttered, some glaring at Geoffrey, others at Maud.

Maud strode to the men. Her bearing was regal despite the mud stains on her hem. She stepped forward, holding her relic high for all to see. Her voice was steady, carrying to every corner. "You doubt? Then look. Here."

She bent low, turning the relic into the candlelight so the lords might see. Her finger traced the base of the wrist, where the gold was smooth.

"The master goldsmith who fashioned the relic on the table before you at my command left his seal on this other one, the true Hand—a cross so fine only close eyes might find it. This mark is the maker's true mark. You can fake gold, but you can't fake a man's secret mark. This is the Hand entrusted to me by the Emperor and his forebears. The other, the one that nearly killed my brave knight, Sir Geoffrey, is the impostor."

Gasps rippled through the assembly. Some craned forward, squinting to see. Others bowed their heads, murmuring prayers.

Geoffrey exhaled, the breath he had held for what seemed like days escaping at last. So she had known. While he bled, while he doubted, while wolves prowled around him, Maud had the true relic with her all along.

Empress Maud turned to her knight. "Sir Geoffrey, forgive my deception, but I could not tell even you that there were two relics. The treachery of the Bishop and his ally John Marshal could just as easily have led them to my tent where the real

Hand of Maud was hidden. Forgive me, Sir Knight."

Geoffrey knelt at her feet and kissed the hem of her cloak. "I would fight and die for even an impostor relic, if that is your wish, my Empress."

"You almost did, my friend. Rise, Sir Knight," she said. Before the assembly, Maud fixed Geoffrey with a steady gaze. "You have stood for me when others fled. You have held my cause as if it were your own, and in you I find a loyalty I can trust above all others. By my right as daughter of a king and heir to his crown, I name you my Justiciar—the arm of my justice and the keeper of my peace. Where I cannot sit in judgment, you shall sit for me. Where my word cannot be spoken, yours shall carry its weight."

The Bishop spat a curse, his hands trembling. Guards swept the Hand of Maud away from the hall for safekeeping.

Geoffrey rose and his gaze lingered on John Marshal, who watched with narrowed eyes, lips pressed in a thin smile. The fox had failed this time, though Geoffrey, as his nemesis, was led away by the Empress's guards. Yet Geoffrey knew well that men like John Marshal never ceased their scheming.

The true Hand gleamed beneath the torches. And with it, Maud's claim to the crown burned brighter.

CHAPTER TEN

A Queen in All but Name

The war of the cousins did not end with a trumpet but with exhaustion. The poor continued to starve while the rich ate well and hid in stone castles.

At Lincoln, in the harsh February of 1141, Stephen was taken in battle—hauled off in chains while Maud's banners flew high in a cold wind. In London there was the pelting of stones instead of Hosannas. Winchester saw the rout that cost Robert's freedom and bought her one more winter alive after he traded his freedom for hers.

In London that same summer, Maud was on the verge of a coronation, but the city turned on her. Merchants and peasants pelted her allies with stones, and she fled before the crown could touch her head.

In September came the Rout of Winchester, and Robert of Gloucester, her half-brother and right hand, was captured, buying her escape with his liberty. The winter of 1142 saw her pinned at Oxford while the ice dammed the river, allowing Maud to slip away in a white cloak and fur boots like an apparition across the snowy landscape.

The war staggered on. In the end, it was not victory that settled England, but a bargain struck among men too tired to bury more sons. At Wallingford in 1153, oaths were remade: Stephen would keep his crown while he lived, but he would name Maud's son as his heir. It was a strange triumph—won without the anointing oil that had seemed her destiny—but a triumph nonetheless. And Maud finally relented.

She returned to Normandy and married Geoffrey of Anjou, a loving and patient husband. Their son, Henry, grew into a man with an iron will that matched his mother's and an ambition that would, in time, expand the English territory well into France. In 1154, he took the crown as Henry II, first of the Plantagenet kings, with the famed Eleanor of Aquitaine beside him. Between them, they would control half a continent. From them came a brood of children whose names would never be forgotten—some for good, and one for ill: Richard the Lionheart, a warrior king, and his brother John, ruthless, a man who could not keep the lands and treasure he was given.

Throughout those years, the true Hand of Maud lay in the royal treasury, recorded by clerks, blessed by priests, displayed to lords on rare occasions. Kings carried it in processions and queens touched it for a blessing.

But relics cannot save men from themselves.

CHAPTER ELEVEN

A Legacy of Honor

The fire burned low in the hearth, its glow casting long shadows across the hall. Sir Geoffrey de Morville, Justiciar of England, sat in his chair, his shoulders wrapped in wool against the bite of winter. His hair was white now, his body worn from years of war and service, yet his eyes still held the steel of a knight who had sworn oaths and kept them.

At his feet sat a boy of nine, wide-eyed and eager. Alfred, his grandson, clutched a wooden sword as if it were real. He had begged for a story—not of kings or saints, but of the night Geoffrey had ridden through storm and treachery to guard the Hand of Maud.

Geoffrey's voice was quiet but steady. "Remember this, boy: treasure is nothing—not gold, not jewels, not even relics. What matters is the oath you give, and the honor you keep. That is a knight's true wealth."

Alfred leaned closer, his face lit by the fire. "Were you ever afraid, Grandfather?"

Geoffrey's smile was faint, touched with weariness. "Every man knows fear. The question is whether fear rules him, or he rules fear. One day, you will learn the difference."

The boy's wooden blade tapped restlessly against the floor. Geoffrey watched him, and memory stirred: another child, laughing in a king's camp, brandishing a stick like a knight's sword. Young William Marshal—John Marshal's son—a hostage then, spirited and playful.

Geoffrey's gaze softened. "There is a young man in this realm, older than you. William is his name. If God wills it, you may one day stand at his side. He has already become a knight making his name in the lists. He may one day be the greatest knight England shall ever know. And you, Alfred, must be steadfast enough to keep faith with him."

"But Grandfather," said Alfred. "You're the greatest knight who ever lived. How can there be another?"

Geoffrey smiled at Alfred. "There's room for two great knights, isn't there?"

Alfred grinned, swinging his stick in the air like a sword. Geoffrey laid a weathered hand on his head and blessed him silently.

The fire crackled. The wind pressed against the shutters. For a moment, Geoffrey felt peace.

The Hand of Maud lay through the years—in war and peace, in plenty and famine—locked away. But Geoffrey knew the relic was only ever a symbol. The true treasure was in the passing of honor from one generation to the next.

And somewhere in England, another man, no longer a cheerful boy—bold, fearless William—was growing toward a destiny that would outshine relics and kings alike.

CHAPTER TWELVE

The Meeting of Alfred and William

The lists outside London thrummed with noise—the clang of metal against metal, the bellow of heralds, the restless stamping of destriers as young knights waited their turn to prove themselves. Alfred de Morville shouldered his way through the press, a young man of fifteen, broad-shouldered but untested, his grandfather's sword at his side, though he had never drawn it in anger.

At the far end of the tiltyard, a tall figure in worn chainmail adjusted the straps on his horse's tack. His coat was plain, with no arms upon it, but there was a steadiness in the set of his shoulders. Alfred overheard another squire whisper, "That one—William, the younger son. He rides for nothing but honor, for he has no inheritance. His father was the marshal of England, but he fell into scandal. One day young William will inherit the title, no doubt."

The trumpet sounded. William lowered his lance, his charger leapt forward, and with a crack like thunder he unhorsed a knight twice his girth. The crowd roared. William landed lightly from the saddle to bow to the crowd, and when his eyes lifted, they met Alfred's across the field.

Later, among the tents, Alfred found himself summoned. William stood before him, helm tucked under one arm, his hair damp with sweat.

"You carry yourself well," William said. "Whose blood are you?"

"Geoffrey de Morville's grandson, my lord," Alfred answered, voice steady despite the heat in his cheeks. "I was told to learn service before I learn arms."

William studied him for a long moment. Then he held out his gauntlet. "Serve me, then," William said, palm open, eyes bright. "If you're half your grandsire, I'll count myself rich indeed. The name of Sir Geoffrey de Morville is legend."

Alfred clasped the offered hand, and in that moment felt the weight of his family's past—Geoffrey who had fought John Marshal, and now himself, bound in service to John's son. The wheel of fortune had turned.

From that day, Alfred tended William's armor, kept his horses, and stood at his stirrup. And as he watched his master ride down foe after foe, Alfred's heart bound itself to William's cause. If William the Marshal was to climb from landless knight to the greatest lord in Christendom, Alfred would be by his side all the way.

EPILOGUE

The Hand of Maud lay through the years—war and peace, starvation and abundance—serenely in the royal treasury, locked in an oak chest and protected by fierce castle guards. Scribes recorded it, priests blessed it, kings paraded it with their regalia. It was said to bring God's favor to the crown.

But to Sir Geoffrey, who had fought and bled for it, the relic was a warning. Time proved him right. In the year 1216, King John—Empress Maud's grandson, the last son of Henry II—fled across the marshes of the Wash, hounded by rebellion from his barons and war with France. His baggage train sank beneath the tide, swallowing gold, jewels, and treasures of the crown. Among them was the Hand of Maud, lost forever in the mire.

They say the tide took it. That the Wash keeps what it eats. So the chroniclers say.

Yet Sir Geoffrey de Morville, very old by then, had known from the first that such a relic could never simply vanish. Too many oaths had been sworn upon it. Too much blood had been shed for it.

And perhaps one day—by means no man could yet imagine—a stranger from another age would find it again.

If this glimpse into the world of Empress Matilda—commonly known as Empress Maud—has captured your imagination, the story is only just beginning.

The legacy of the Hand reawakens with the struggle for power and destiny in *The Hand of Maud*—where time itself yields to its mystery.

And beyond, the saga continues in *Heir to the Hand*, coming in 2026.

Scan this QR code to step into *The Hand of Maud*, where the legacy deepens.

Don't miss the sequel, *Heir to the Hand*, arriving in 2026.

Please enjoy the following excerpt from *The Hand of Maud*.

PROLOGUE

Bouvines, France
1214

Eleanor's eyes fluttered against a bright sun. A sudden sun. It was dark one moment, and bright the next. Strange noises chittered all around.

I must have fainted. So many voices, buzzing, anxious, moaning, yelling.

How did I get here? I was at the medieval fair with my friend Carol. July. The fair commemorating the Battle of Bouvines. That's right; I remember now. My name is Eleanor MacLean. The year is 1964, and I was watching a magic show at the fair. I stepped into the magic tent. The strange magician looming in the shadows. The curtain wrapped around me like a shroud. His dead, black eyes, bottomless, staring. The air thickened. Dizzy...

... The world began to tilt.

Eleanor's head—or the ground, she couldn't tell—spun in wild, frantic loops. Arms outstretched, flailing, she grasped at nothing as she fell. Then she realized she was already on the ground. Her stomach lurched, and she vomited in the dirt. She rolled onto her back, waiting for the spinning to stop, eyes closed. Stretched out, pale, sweating, panting, she slowly began to recover and turned her attention to the sounds around her.

She opened her eyes. To her right, several men were lying on the ground, re-enacting a battle scene, typical of medieval re-enactments. Horses in the distance charged at each other, swords clashing, and one knight fell to the ground. So realistic.

She watched with fascination, lifting herself sluggishly onto one elbow to see better.

How real it looks. But how did I get here? Why am I on the ground?

I was in the magician's tent. I don't remember walking to the jousting arena. Where's Carol? Something must've made me sick. I must've fainted.

A noise to her left. She rolled over onto her other elbow to view the re-enactment from the other side and gasped in horror. She was lying next to a dying man. She corrected herself: a man pretending to be dying. He moaned and cupped his hands over his wound. It looked so convincing that she recoiled from the gruesome scene. He was lying on his back, a huge gash on his side oozing red, seeping between his fingers.

How did he make it look so real? And why was she on the ground in the middle of this re-enactment? What had happened to the fairgrounds?

Looking around, she could only see the battlefield where the re-enactment was taking place, not the fair that should have been visible all around with its flags and tents, the vendors, the booths, the salesmen hawking medieval garb and trinkets, the girls dressed as wenches. They were all gone.

What was happening? It was as if the world had tilted off its axis and she couldn't find her footing.

The dying man looked at her with an imploring, pleading look. Ragged breathing. His face was pale gray, and his eyes were moist, shadowed with red streaks. Great acting. But the man would not stop staring at her as he played out the death scene. Finally, he stopped groaning and panting and appeared to stop breathing altogether. His eyes ceased to see her, although they were still open. He didn't blink. *Please blink. Please, please blink.* But he didn't. *I must be imagining it.*

She struggled to her feet but wobbled and slid onto her knees. She was dizzy and weak again and wanted to get back to the hotel where she and Carol had been staying. *If I could only lie on the bed for a while, I'd feel better.* She could not look at the battle re-enactment without feeling queasy, so she covered her face with her hands, crouching into a small, round ball, while the battle, the mock battle, raged about her.

Think, Ellie, think. Try to remember how you got here. Think...

Her mind swirled, like water running down a drain, gaining no traction. Then the ground began to shake in rhythmic beats, like a subterranean drumbeat rising nearer and nearer to the surface. She looked up toward the noise. A man on a white horse—a huge white horse with powerful hindquarters and a broad chest—was galloping toward her. He stopped only feet away with a quick, sharp jerk of the reins. The horse reared up on its hind legs.

The man dressed as a knight and the horse were covered in chain-mail armor. He was a tall, powerful man, well built with broad, muscled shoulders. He was sturdy and well seated on the horse. His head was also covered in a helmet of chain mail, but his face was visible. His hair, sprinkled with gray, created a fringe at the front of his helmet. He had a gray close-cropped beard and brilliant eyes set in a weathered but handsome face. He was an older man, imposing. He carried a shield and a sword, which he held in the air poised as if he would slice down on her neck at any moment.

"Woman," he said, addressing her in a deep, forceful voice, "what are ye doing here in this place of battle? It's no place for a young woman like yerself. Get up, get up now, I say!"

What language was he speaking? It sounded like French, which she could speak but only with difficulty. She vaguely grasped his meaning yet couldn't find the words to reply. Why was one of the jousters trying to draw her into the re-enactment, especially when she was obviously so sick? Did he think she was part of the show? Looking up at him, his fearsome tone, his angry eyes, and the snorting horse that looked like it could stomp her head into the ground with one strong kick, she felt dizzy and fainted.

Some time later—she could not tell how much time had

passed—her mind came swimming back to consciousness. She was bouncing along on the back end of the galloping horse, slung over sideways, face down toward the ground. The knight's woven armor dug into her bare flesh. She started to scream and finally found her voice. "Stop! Where are you taking me? Stop, please!"

The knight reined in the horse quickly, and with one arm reached around, gripped Eleanor by the waist and swung her up into a sitting position behind him astride the horse. "Hold on," he commanded in English. "We need to get away from here."

She obeyed, and wrapped her arms around his broad waist, clinging to the metal armor. It scraped her exposed skin again, and she winced. His sword had been holstered in its scabbard, on the left side of his body, so she gripped its handle to help steady her as he led the horse into a full gallop.

As the horse and its two passengers raced away from the battlefield, Eleanor cast a look back at the scene she had just escaped. Dozens of bodies, maybe hundreds, were writhing and moaning on the ground. She had never witnessed such a vivid, frightening re-enactment. As the field grew smaller with distance, the fallen reminded her of insects caught on flypaper, wriggling and fighting for their lives, a ghastly pantomime of the moments before death.

This was real, she thought. *If I'm not dreaming, this is all real.*

But she quickly put the thought out of her mind as she, the knight, and the horse raced away from the battlefield and into the forest edging the field of carnage.

Excerpt from The Hand of Maud:

CHAPTER ONE

Eleanor

Eleanor was thinking about her granddaughter when the power went out.

It was almost time to go to bed when the TV made a zizz-ing sound and went black. The lights flashed a few times, then stayed off.

She was in the kitchen shuffling around in her slippers and old bathrobe. She had just put the water on for a cup of tea when the power died. "Darn it," she muttered. The kettle's whistle faded away like a dying siren, but the water was hot enough, so she poured it into a cup and let the tea steep while she hunted for candles.

There they were, in the back of the junk drawer. Placing some candles around the house, she walked back into the kitchen and turned on her radio—the fancy radio her granddaughter, Donna, had given her.

"Grandma, you can listen to the radio on the internet now," she'd told her. "Or on your phone. You don't need to have a separate radio."

"Dumplin', I can't be bothered to turn on the computer every time I want to hear the news, and it sounds too small and too tinny on my phone."

She turned on the radio, and the Beach Boys started singing "Help Me, Rhonda." Eleanor began to move with the music, bopping up and down, side to side. Then she caught sight of herself in the dining room mirror—her 80-year-old self— dancing in her frayed pink bathrobe and fuzzy slippers, sipping on a cup of old granny tea, and she laughed.

She took another sip and tuned the radio to local news. There was no information on the power outage. Then she tuned the dial to her favorite news station, BBC. She had a keen interest in news from England.

While the announcer droned on about the latest excesses of the Parliament, Eleanor continued pondering her granddaughter's future. *What will Donna do when she graduates from college? And when I'm gone, what will happen to her? She'll have this house, but I hope I live long enough to see her find someone, get married, have children, and live on her own. I want her married and safe before I die.*

That thought made her laugh again. *Safe? Back then? Not even remotely. And yet, here I am.*

Donna will be home soon from the campus library. I'll try to wait up, tell her about the power outage. Make sure she eats something. This was their routine when Donna worked late.

Suddenly her ears perked up. The BBC announcer was saying something that made her stop dead. Scalding water sloshed over the side of her cup as she halted mid-step, burning her skin, but she didn't flinch. She stood motionless, like a statue—like one of Pompeii's doomed, frozen in the middle of an ordinary moment.

"The long-lost treasure of King John, who lost the crown jewels of England in 1216 as he attempted to cross marshy ground off the coast of England, may have been unearthed by a metal detectorist who has scanned a farm in a Lincolnshire village," the announcer said. "Peter Foster Hughes, sixty-three, says he is one-hundred percent certain that the 800-plus-year-old artifacts he has located at an undisclosed site did, indeed, belong to the former King of England—who was often described as the evilest monarch in British history. Hughes's equipment has isolated what he calls high-value items he believes include gold, silver, emeralds, sapphires, and rubies."

Then the voice of metal detectorist Peter Foster Hughes crackled over the radio. "People have been searching for the lost crown jewels for centuries, and I'm certain we've located them."

He spoke in a rapid, breathless tone. "If we can bring them up, we may finally recover some of the spectacular crowns and jewelry worn by the royal family, including magnificent relics like the Hand of Maud."

What was wrong with her feet? Eleanor could not move. Her breathing became rapid, like that of Peter Foster Hughes breathlessly recounting his discovery. She started to pant. She forced herself to snap out of her trance, lunged for the radio, and cranked up the volume. Grabbing a pen from the half open junk drawer, she began writing down details of the news report on her tea-stained napkin.

She sat on the sofa in the dark living room minutes later. The only light came from the flickering candle on the coffee table. The napkin with her scribbles lay on her lap, as her mind raced in circles, reliving a horrifying event from her past. The wet, musty smell of mud, mingling with the sound of men screaming and gasping for breath. The horses, shrieking and flailing their legs, their large nostrils flared, desperate for air. Her thoughts clawed at her mind, like an undertow dragging the past into the future. She pressed both hands to the sides of her head and closed her eyes, as if trying to squeeze out some semblance of calm and reason.

They found them. They really did. After eight centuries... they're finally found. What do I do? Should I call this man in England and tell him what I know? Should I tell him...

The lights flickered and came back on.

**Continue the Story by reading
The Hand of Maud, available now**

Thank you for reading *The First Betrayal*

www.ingramcontent.com/pod-product-compliance
Lightning Source LLC
Chambersburg PA
CBHW070354130626
46556CB00007B/3168